Little GODDESS Girls

Persephone & the Unicorn's Ruby

JOAN HOLUB & SUZANNE WILLIAMS

ALADDIN QUIX

New York London Toronto Sydney New Delhi

ALADDIN QUIX

Simon & Schuster Children's Publishing Division

1230 Avenue of the Americas, New York, New York 10020

First Aladdin paperback edition May 2022

Text copyright © 2022 by Joan Holub and Suzanne Williams

Illustrations copyright © 2022 by Yuyi Chen

Also available in an Aladdin QUIX hardcover edition.

All rights reserved, including the right of reproduction in whole or in part in any form.

ALADDIN and the related marks and colophon are trademarks of Simon & Schuster, Inc.

For information about special discounts for bulk purchases, please contact Simon & Schuster Special Sales at 1-866-506-1949 or business@simonandschuster.com.

The Simon & Schuster Speakers Bureau can bring authors to your live event. For more information or to book an event contact the Simon & Schuster Speakers Bureau at 1-866-248-3049 or visit our website at www.simonspeakers.com.

Designed by Tiara Iandiorio

The illustrations for this book were rendered digitally.

The text of this book was set in Archer.

Manufactured in the United States of America 0322 OFF

2 4 6 8 10 9 7 5 3 1

Library of Congress Control Number 2021945036

ISBN 978-1-6659-0408-7 (hc)

ISBN 978-1-6659-0407-0 (pbk)

ISBN 978-1-6659-0409-4 (ebook)

Welcome to ALADDIN QUIX!

If you are looking for fast, fun-to-read stories with colorful characters, lots of kid-friendly humor, easy-to-follow action, entertaining story lines, and lively illustrations, then **ALADDIN QUIX** is for you!

But wait, there's more!

If you're also looking for stories with tables of contents; word lists; about-the-book questions; 64, 80, or 96 pages; short chapters; short paragraphs; and large fonts, then **ALADDIN QUIX** is *definitely* for you!

ALADDIN QUIX: The next step between ready to reads and longer, more challenging chapter books, for readers five to eight years old.

Read more ALADDIN QUIX books!

By Stephanie Calmenson

Our Principal Is a Frog!
Our Principal Is a Wolf!
Our Principal's in His Underwear!
Our Principal Breaks a Spell!
Our Principal's Wacky Wishes!

Royal Sweets
By Helen Perelman

Book 1: *A Royal Rescue*
Book 2: *Sugar Secrets*
Book 3: *Stolen Jewels*
Book 4: *The Marshmallow Ghost*
Book 5: *Chocolate Challenge*

A Miss Mallard Mystery
By Robert Quackenbush

Dig to Disaster
Texas Trail to Calamity
Express Train to Trouble
Stairway to Doom
Bicycle to Treachery
Gondola to Danger
Surfboard to Peril
Taxi to Intrigue

Little Goddess Girls
By Joan Holub and Suzanne Williams

Book 1: *Athena & the Magic Land*
Book 2: *Persephone & the Giant Flowers*
Book 3: *Aphrodite & the Gold Apple*
Book 4: *Artemis & the Awesome Animals*
Book 5: *Athena & the Island Enchantress*
Book 6: *Persephone & the Evil King*
Book 7: *Aphrodite & the Magical Box*
Book 8: *Artemis & the Wishing Kitten*

Cast of Characters

Persephone (purr•SEFF•uh•nee): Red-haired Greek goddess of plants and flowers

Aphrodite (af•row•DIE•tee): Golden-haired Greek goddess of love and beauty

Hestia (HESS•tee•uh): A small, winged Greek goddess, who helps Athena and her friends

Zeus (ZOOSS): Most powerful of the Greek gods, who lives in Sparkle City and can grant wishes

Adonis (uh•DAHN•niss): A cute white bunny boy wearing a rainbow ribbon

What-Ifs (wuht•IFFS): Fearful bunnies that live in a castle in East Mount Olympus

Cut-Ups (CUT•upps): Characters that live in a kingdom in South Mount Olympus

unicorn (YOO•nih•corn): A horselike creature with a tall horn on its head

King Bunny (KING BUHN•nee): Ruler of the Castle of What-Ifs

Contents

1

Treasure Hunt

"I see it! I see the signpost!" called **Persephone.** She bounced on her toes in excitement. "The Hello Brick Road splits into two directions up ahead!"

"Yay! I see it too,"

said her friend **Aphrodite**.

They both ran up the Hello Brick Road toward the signpost. The road was made of orange, blue, and pink bricks. It led to places all over **Mount Olympus**— this magic land where the two girls lived. Right now, they hoped the road would lead them to a treasure. Two stolen **jewels**!

Persephone reached the sign-post first. Her curly red hair swung around her shoulders as she came to a sudden stop.

Oops! She'd stopped so fast that Aphrodite bumped into her from behind. The small crown Aphrodite wore atop her shiny golden hair fell off. And Persephone dropped her silver cane. It had been given to her by **Hestia**, a tiny flying **goddess**. It was magic!

Persephone caught the crown before it could hit the ground. She handed it back to her friend. **"That was a lucky catch!** Thanks," Aphrodite said as she put on her crown.

Persephone grinned and patted the four-leaf clovers that grew in her hair. They were the same color as her green eyes. "Yeah, good thing **Zeus** gave me these lucky clovers. Without them I probably couldn't have caught it!"

Zeus was a boy about eight years old—the same age as both girls. Yet he was the super-duper powerful king of the Greek **gods**!

Not long ago, he'd given Persephone the gift of good luck. This made her even better at a magical skill she'd always had—growing plants. In addition to the clovers, flowers grew in her hair. And on her dress!

Aphrodite's crown had been a gift from Zeus too. It was not only pretty. It also helped her remember to think before she said things that might hurt others' feelings.

Persephone glanced up at the signpost again. One sign pointed east. It read: TO THE CASTLE OF WHAT-IFS. The other pointed south. It read: TO THE KINGDOM OF CUT-UPS.

She looked over at Aphrodite. "Which way should we go first?"

"Ooh! Pick me!" said the What-Ifs sign.

"No! Pick me!" said the Cut-Ups sign.

Persephone grinned. Here in Mount Olympus, many objects and creatures could speak!

"Give us a minute to think," she told the signs. She wondered if **Athena** or **Artemis** had found any jewels yet. They were Aphrodite's and Persephone's other two best friends, who were also searching for treasure. The girls had all first met a few weeks ago. And they'd already had lots of fun and magical adventures together since then!

Aphrodite looked both ways. Then she said to Persephone, "Maybe we

to the
CASTLE
of
WHAT-IFS

to the
KINGDOM
of
CUT-UPS

should split up? That way, we could each go down a different road to hunt for both jewels at the same time."

All four friends had begun their treasure quests earlier that morning, after a **mermaid statue** had asked Athena for help. Help in finding four jewels—a missing **pearl**, **ruby**, **emerald**, and **diamond**! Each had been stolen from Thunderbolt Tower. Which was where Zeus lived in Sparkle City, high atop Mount Olympus.

The mermaid knew who the thieves were—Four Magic Winds! The East Wind had whisked away the ruby and hidden it in the East. The South Wind had blown the emerald to the South. So Persephone and Aphrodite had come here, hoping to find them.

Meanwhile, Athena was hunting for the mermaid's black pearl in the North. It had been whirled away by the North Wind. And Artemis had gone west, because the West Wind had huff-puffed the diamond there.

"It would be more fun to stick together," Persephone said. She missed their other two friends and didn't want to go off by herself.

"But splitting up would save time," said Aphrodite.

Before they could agree on a plan, a sweet little voice spoke to them. "Hello. My name is **Adonis Bunnyboy.**"

"Huh?" said Persephone. She saw no one up ahead.

"Look down," Aphrodite

said to her. To both girls' surprise, a snow-white bunny with blue eyes was hopping around their feet! He wore a rainbow-colored ribbon tied into a bow at his neck. The best way to make friends on the Hello Brick Road was to say hello to someone. This bunny must want to be friends!

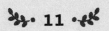

2

Cutest Bunny Ever

"Hello, Adonis. I'm Persephone," Persephone told the white bunny.

"And I'm Aphrodite. I like your ribbon!" said Aphrodite.

Adonis smiled. "Thanks." The bunny stood up on his two back legs and looked at them both. "You are the biggest bunnies I've ever seen!"

Persephone laughed. "We're not bunnies at all. We're girls. Girl goddesses."

It was true! Hestia had told them so. Persephone, Aphrodite, Artemis, and Athena were still learning how to use their powers, though.

"Are you lost?" Aphrodite asked the bunny.

"Yes," the bunny said shyly. "I'm trying to find my way back to the Castle of What-Ifs. That's where I live."

"You're in luck!" said Persephone. "Because we're heading there on a treasure hunt. Right, Aphrodite?" She was sure her friend would change her mind about splitting up now. And she was right.

"Your castle is that way," Aphrodite said, pointing east. "We'll go with you to make sure you get home."

Yay! thought Persephone. Treasure hunting with a friend would be way more fun than doing it alone.

The bunny wiggled his cute pink nose. **"Goody!"** He hopped up and down. Then he asked, "What's a treasure hunt?"

"It means we're hunting for jewels," Persephone explained, as the three of them headed east.

"The king of The Castle of What-Ifs has a crown with jewels," said Adonis.

"Really? Is one of the jewels a red ruby?" asked Aphrodite, sounding excited.

Adonis stopped hopping and wiggled his nose, thinking. "I don't remember."

Persephone bent down to pat the bunny. Aphrodite did too. Its fur was supersoft. *Mmm*. And he smelled really nice. Like chocolate and candy sprinkles.

Adonis looked from Persephone to Aphrodite and back. To their surprise, he said, "I like you. Can I be your pet?"

Was he asking *her*? Persephone wondered. Or Aphrodite? She wasn't sure. But right then and there, she fell in love with the bunny. He was so sweet and cute! She'd never had her own pet before.

"You can be my pet," Persephone and Aphrodite said at the exact same time.

Uh-oh! Aphrodite must like the bunny as much as I do, Persephone thought. She felt a little pain in her heart. *Would the bunny like Aphrodite better?*

The bunny didn't say whose pet he wanted to be. Instead, he just said, **"Okay! C'mon!"** And he began hopping happily along the East Road again.

Aphrodite glanced over at Persephone as they hurried to catch up with Adonis. "You're probably too busy taking care of your plants to take care of a bunny," she said.

"No, I'm not," Persephone replied. "And since bunnies eat plants and I grow them, I can make sure he gets plenty of good food."

Aphrodite was quiet. "Well, I saw Adonis first," she finally said. "So it's only fair that I get to keep him." She began to walk faster.

Persephone went faster too. Adonis hopped quicker than they could walk, so he still stayed ahead of them.

"**No fair!** It doesn't matter who saw him first!" Persephone's cheeks turned pink with anger. Which was weird, since she hardly ever got mad. But suddenly she found herself wishing that she and her friend *had* split up. And that Aphrodite had gone south!

Hearing them, the bunny stopped. Its whiskers twitched in **alarm**. *"Eek!* Are you two going to fight? I don't like fighting. What if you start pushing each other? You could fall on top of me. I might get squished!" Adonis sped up his hops, in a hurry to get away from them now.

Up ahead What-Ifs Castle came into view. It had four tall walls with a fancy tower at each corner, but no roof. At its center, a tall, twisted pole poked up toward the sky.

The bunny peeked at them over his shoulder. "Stop following so close! What if you step on my tail?"

"Don't worry. I'll be careful," said Persephone. This little bunny was turning out to be a bit of a

scaredy-cat. But that didn't make her like him any less.

"Me too," Aphrodite added.

"If you stepped on my tail, it would hurt," the bunny went on. "Then I might have to go to the doctor. **Boo-hoo!**" he wailed as he hop, hop, hopped.

"Calm down. If your tail was long, I suppose someone might step on it by **accident**. But it's short," said Aphrodite. "So that won't happen."

Adonis's blue eyes got wide.

"But what if it wasn't short? Would you step on it then?"

Aphrodite sent him a sweet smile. "I promise I won't step on your tail."

"Me too," Persephone quickly said. She didn't want Aphrodite to outdo her. Then Adonis might like her better.

"Well, okay," said the bunny. His hops slowed a bit. But a minute later he said, "What if a bear jumps out from the trees and trips you? Would you fall on me then?"

Persephone huffed and spread her arms wide and looked all around. "I don't see any bears here. **Do you?**"

Adonis also looked around. "What if they're **invisible**?"

Aphrodite let out a giggle. "More like *imaginary*."

Just then, they arrived at the Castle of What-Ifs. Adonis hopped in through its two big wooden doors.

The What-Ifs

The girls followed and Persephone sniffed the air inside the castle. **"Wow!** It smells *sooo* good in here!"

Aphrodite took a sniff too. "*Mmm.* It does!"

"That's because the castle is built out of chocolate, and it's full of yummy snacks," Adonis explained. "But be careful. There's danger everywhere."

"Really?" said Persephone, looking around. Many busy bunnies of different colors and sizes were all hopping here and there. And, except for the bunnies, everything really was made of snacks!

Small houses sat all along each of the castle's four tall chocolate walls. She pointed at them. "Those houses are built out of ginger-bread! And their roofs are made of marshmallows!"

Aphrodite pointed down at the stepping-stones they were walking over. "And these stones are peppermints!"

Creak-creak! Right then a cart with cookie wheels rolled by. A blue bunny was driving it. It waved and smiled at them, showing big white teeth.

"Danger! Danger!" said Adonis. He leaped into

Persephone's arms. "See what I mean? What if that cart had run over me?"

Persephone and Aphrodite grinned at each other. The cart hadn't come anywhere near Adonis. But then they remembered their battle over the bunny. Quickly, their grins became frowns.

Once the cart had passed,

Adonis jumped to the ground again. "See you later," he said. Then he hopped over to see his bunny friends.

The girls walked farther into the castle.

"Look!" Persephone waved her hand toward a large white unicorn statue that stood in a fountain at the center of the castle. Its glittery, twisty horn pointed up at the sky. It was the same pointed tip they'd seen poking up from the castle on the way here!

As Aphrodite walked closer, her blue eyes went wide. "I think this statue is made of white chocolate! And the water in this fountain is chocolate milk!"

Persephone grinned at Aphrodite and rubbed her stomach. **"Yum!**

I'm starting to get hungry." Now that the bunny wasn't with them, they weren't fighting over him. That was good. Her friends were super important to her. She only had three of them and didn't want to lose one!

Aphrodite nodded. "Me too!"

Right then Persephone had an idea. "Hey, remember how Athena said that fountain mermaid statue she met could talk? I wonder if this unicorn statue talks too."

"And maybe it knows where the

ruby is?" Aphrodite's eyes shone with excitement. The two girls leaned over the edge of the fountain toward the statue.

"Psst. **Unicorn!** Can you talk?" asked Persephone.

The unicorn didn't answer.

Aphrodite sighed in disappointment. "Oh, well, it was a worth a try."

"Why are you talking to that statue?" Adonis asked. He had hopped up behind them without them noticing. "What if talking to it made something bad happen?

Like what if it started snorting fire and burned down the castle?"

"I don't think unicorns snort fire. You must be thinking of dragons," Persephone said kindly.

A cute green-and-white-spotted bunny hopped up to them. "Did you say d-d-dragons?" it asked in a shaky voice.

"Yes, but don't worry. There aren't any dragons here," Aphrodite assured it.

More bunnies gathered around them.

"But what if dragons hear us talking about them and that makes them come?" asked a purple bunny. It shivered with fear.

It seemed that all the bunnies here were worriers, not just Adonis, Persephone decided. While the bunnies continued to chat about

the terrible things that dragons might do, the two girls tiptoed away to search for the ruby.

They stopped in front of the biggest house within the castle walls. It had more candy decorations than the others. Gumdrops covered its roof. The fence around it was made of cinnamon sticks.

But the garden was the best part. Persephone clapped her hands in delight. "Wow, look! There are lemon drops, candy corn, and jelly beans growing here. And the dirt isn't dirt. **It's melted chocolate!**"

Just then, a large bunny ran out of the grand house toward them. He stood on two paws instead of four, making him almost as tall as the girls. His clothes were super fancy and he wore a crown.

"Look! That crown has jewels in it!" Persephone whispered to Aphrodite.

They hurried over to the big bunny. Up close they could see that the crown's jewels were pink,

yellow, and blue, with a big brown jewel on top.

Aphrodite frowned with disappointment. "Rubies are *red*."

"Rats," said Persephone. "I'm lucky, but not lucky enough to find that stolen ruby, I guess. Not yet, anyway."

"Help! Help!" the fancy bunny suddenly shouted. "Someone stole my ears!"

Adonis and the other bunnies in the castle raced over at once. They stood in a circle around the fancy bunny. "It's true! Someone has stolen **King Bunny**'s ears!" they shouted.

"My ears! I miss my fluffy ears!" yelled King Bunny. "What if I never get them back?!"

"Did you see who stole them?" an orange bunny asked.

"Did they leave any clues?" a yellow bunny added.

"I *didn't* see. And no clues at all," the king said sadly. "I was just getting ready to go out for a walk. I put on my crown and then looked in the mirror. And my ears were gone!"

The bunnies began to suggest possible thieves. "What if a bald giant stole your ears to make a warm, furry hat?" "What if twin bears took them to wear as neckties?" "What if a monster stole them to make itself a long beard?" Each idea was sillier than the next. "Hey! **I found a clue!**" said a pink bunny. It pointed at the ground. "Footprints! And they lead right to those two girls!"

A blue bunny pointed at Persephone and Aphrodite. "What if *they* stole your ears!"

"Yes! That must be what happened," shouted the other bunnies.

The king frowned at Aphrodite and Persephone. "If you don't give me back my ears, **I'll have to put you in jail!**"

Persephone rolled her eyes. "We didn't steal your ears," she told him. "And I can prove it."

"How?" the king asked.

"Well, can you hear me speak-

ing right now?" Persephone asked.

"Yes," said the king.

Persephone spread her arms wide. "If you didn't have ears, then you couldn't hear me. Right?"

Aphrodite pointed at the king's

head. "Your ears must be under your crown! That's why you can't see them."

"That doesn't make sense!" replied the king. "*You're* wearing a crown, too. But I can still see *your* ears."

The other bunnies hopped around, nodding their agreement. "He's right!"

"No, Aphrodite's right," said Persephone. "I'll show you!" She grabbed the crown from King Bunny's head. Two fluffy ears unfolded to stand straight up. *Boing! Boing!*

The crowd of bunnies cheered.

"You found my ears!" The king smiled big at the girls. "I must give you a reward. Is there anything you want?"

"**Wait!** What if they want to become our new king as a reward?" shouted a bunny.

"Yeah! What if they do become king, and then decide to eat our castle?" shouted another. "Oh, boo-hoo!"

4

Chocolate Unicorn

Persephone sighed. "Don't worry. We don't want to be kings," she told the bunnies.

"Or queens," added Aphrodite.

"We're only here to find a jewel," Persephone said. Her

eyes went to the king's crown.

To her surprise, just then he plucked a yellow jewel off his crown and ate it.

"So, I guess those aren't real jewels, are they?" she asked.

"Nope. They're candy. Mostly jelly beans I picked from my garden," said the king. "Who needs them?"

"We do!" The girls pointed through a large window in the castle wall, toward the top of Mount Olympus.

"Whoa! Sparkle City is covered in fog!" the king shouted. "I can hardly see the tip-top of Thunderbolt Tower!"

Persephone and Aphrodite quickly explained about the Four Winds stealing the jewels. And their quest to find them, so Zeus could make his city **sparkle** again.

Suddenly there was a crack of thunder. ***Ka-boom!*** The bunnies' eyes got big.

"What if that thunder means it's going to rain? It's never rained on our castle before," gasped a black bunny.

"What if it rains . . . what if it rains . . . ," the bunnies all chanted.

"You're afraid of rain?" Persephone asked them in surprise.

"Of course!" said Adonis. "Don't you know what happens to chocolate in the rain? Or to gingerbread? Or marshmallows?"

"They melt?" Persephone and Aphrodite guessed together.

"Into goo!" said the king.

The bunnies began to worry

again. "What if our castle melts into a puddle?" "What if it turns to mush?" "What if we have to rebuild it?" **"Oh, boo-hoo!"**

For once the bunnies' worries weren't imaginary ones. Rain could destroy their castle and their homes, too. That would be terrible!

"How can we help?" Aphrodite asked.

Persephone snapped her fingers. "Our goddess powers! Hestia told us to experiment with them to learn how they work, remember?

I'll try to do a stop-the-rain spell."

She thought for a minute, then

waved the tip of her magic cane

in a circle and chanted:

"Rain, rain, go away.

Bring the sun back out to play!"

But her spell didn't work.

Instead, wind began to

whoosh inside the

castle walls,

blowing

their

hair and

dresses.

Clouds appeared overhead. **_Oh no!_** It seemed to Persephone that she'd only made things worse!

Aphrodite gave her a quick hug. "Good try."

Persephone felt so glad that Aphrodite was here with her. Trying to fight trouble was way better with a friend. "Thanks," she said. "Why don't you try a spell too?"

Before Aphrodite could, though, the girls heard a new voice.

"Psst! Over here!"

"Hey, I think that unicorn statue is talking to us now!" said Aphrodite. They rushed over to it.

Persephone leaned over the edge of the fountain toward the statue. "Um, did you just speak?"

"Yes," said the unicorn. It didn't move its mouth when it spoke. "Sorry, this statue is made of hard chocolate, so I can't nod or anything. I'm only using it to visit."

"So you're really *inside* the statue?" Aphrodite asked.

"That's right. Most days I live in a meadow along the Hello Brick Road. But I can't romp there again until my lost ruby is returned to Thunderbolt Tower."

"*Your* ruby?" Persephone said. "So you're the magical creature it belongs to?"

5

Red Ruby

"Yes! My ruby has got to be hidden in this castle somewhere," the unicorn told them. "But I don't know where. Like I said, I can travel from home to live inside unicorn statues. Also unicorn pictures and toys. But I can't stay long."

"I wish I had magic," said a small voice. It was Adonis. He had overheard the unicorn and hopped over to the fountain. "If I did, I'd stop the rain with just a twitch of my magic whiskers."

"*My* magic is in my horn," the unicorn told him.

Adonis looked up at the twisty, pointed horn atop the unicorn statue's head. "Wow, really? But you're chocolate . . . or at least the statue you're inside of is. What if your horn melts in the rain? What if our castle does? What if *I'm* turned to goo? Oh, boo-hoo!"

"Calm down. I'll make sure that won't happen," the unicorn said in a kind voice.

Whoosh! The wind began to blow harder. The clouds overhead turned dark.

"Uh-oh! What if that's the East Wind blowing a storm our way?" worried Persephone.

"Yeah! What if it's trying to stop us from finding the ruby it stole?"

Aphrodite added. It seemed that they were becoming what-if worriers, too!

Before Persephone could try using her magic cane again, it began to rain.

"Don't worry," said the unicorn. **Swish!** Suddenly, a giant umbrella sprouted from the tip-top of its horn! The umbrella was so wide that it shielded the whole castle and everyone inside it. The unicorn had used its magic to save the day!

After a few minutes, the rain stopped and the sun came out. Nothing had gotten wet! All the bunnies and their homes were safe.

Swish! The unicorn closed its umbrella. "You never know when an umbrella will come in handy," it said. "So I always keep one inside my horn."

Then it began to talk fast. "I have to go soon, but, please, you must find my ruby! All four jewels have to be returned to Thunderbolt Tower by tonight. Otherwise

Zeus will become powerless to protect Sparkle City."

"Yes, we know," said Persephone. "That's why we came here. I promise we'll do everything we can to find it in time."

Aphrodite nodded. "It would be horrible if Sparkle City had no protection. Those wild wind brothers would be able to huff and puff and blow Mount Olympus away!"

"True," said the unicorn. "However, for the jewels' magic to work against them, you must—"

The girls leaned forward, listening. "We must what?"

But the unicorn spoke no more. It had already magically left.

The king came up to Aphrodite, Persephone, and Adonis just then. **"We're saved!"** he cheered. He slipped off his crown and waved in it the air. His tall ears twirled around happily.

"Hey!" said Persephone. "The big candy on the top of your crown used to be brown. Now it's red!"

She and Aphrodite stared at the

candy more closely. It was shiny, hard, and more beautiful than any jelly bean. "It's the ruby!" they shouted at the same time.

The king's eyes got wide. "It is? I found that thing a few days ago when I was digging in my garden. I thought it was a chocolate covered cherry, and I licked the chocolate off it just now."

"No, it's the ruby we've been looking for!" Persephone exclaimed. "The East Wind must have blown it into the chocolate dirt in your garden to hide it."

"Can we have it?" said Aphrodite.

"Sure, I can't eat a ruby. I'll just replace it on my crown with a lemon drop," said the king. He gave them the ruby. "Want some jelly beans? You must be hungry." He gave the girls a basket and let them pick some from his garden.

They placed the ruby safely inside the basket with the candies. It was time to go now.

What about Adonis? Whose pet will he be when we all three leave the castle? Persephone wondered. She had a feeling Aphrodite was wondering the same thing.

"Share to be fair," whispered a tiny voice. It came from their basket!

Aphrodite and Persephone looked at each other. "Did that ruby just speak?" asked Aphrodite.

"Yes, it must have! I heard it too," Persephone replied. And suddenly she knew how to make things right. So did Aphrodite.

"What if we share Adonis?" they said at the same time.

"That's a good what-if!" said Adonis, smiling at them. "You

can *both* take care of me. We can all play. **It'll be awesome pawsome.** C'mon, I'll take you to my house. You might not fit, though. We'll have to build two more rooms for you."

"We can't stay. We thought you'd come with us!" said Persephone.

Adonis's blue eyes got big. "Me? Leave the castle forever? But I thought you'd take care of me *here*."

"We can't," Aphrodite told him. "We have to go find another jewel—an emerald."

Persephone nodded. "It's in the Kingdom of Cut-Ups. And after that, we'll need to take both jewels to Thunderbolt Tower where they belong. Only then will Sparkle City sparkle again."

Adonis's eyes got bigger. "A trip like that sounds dangerous."

Persephone knelt beside the cute bunny. "It'll be an adventure. You don't have to come, but we'd love it if you did."

"We're goddesses," Aphrodite reminded him. "We're not that

good at magic spells yet, but we promise to try to keep you safe."

"But what if we come to a crossroads? What if you each grab one of my ears and pull me a different way? What if you stretch

them in different directions? What if they pop off?" the bunny asked in a small, fearful voice.

"We'd never do that," Persephone told him.

"Cross our hearts," said Aphrodite.

However, Adonis was still worried. Several more bunnies had overheard and now gathered around him, coming up with more what-ifs. "What if you go with these girls and you meet a crocodile? What if it snaps you up in his jaws and eats you? Or what if . . . ?"

Persephone elbowed Aphrodite. "Know what I think?" she whispered to her friend. "I think

Adonis might feel happier here!"

"I think you're right!" Aphrodite whispered back. "So *what if* we let him stay, and we go look for the emerald?"

Persephone smiled, even though she was a bit sad to leave Adonis behind. **"Yes, let's do it."**

After saying goodbye to all the bunnies, the girls left the castle. And swinging the basket between them, they began to walk along the Hello Brick Road again.

6

Happy Hugs

Persephone and Aphrodite were super hungry by now. Good thing they had the yummy jelly beans! Once they finished all the candy, Persephone put the ruby in her pocket.

This time, when they reached the signpost, they turned south. Far ahead of them stood the Kingdom of Cut-Ups.

Would they find the emerald there? What if they didn't?

Persephone worried. *Uh-oh!* Had those boo-hoo bunnies' what-if way of thinking rubbed off on her? But then all at once a puff of happiness surrounded her. And it instantly calmed her worries.

"Did you feel that?" she asked Aphrodite. "It felt like a friendly hug came to me from far away."

Aphrodite smiled at her. "**Yes! I felt it too.** I think Athena and Artemis each must have sent us a happy hug-wish! I hope they're both doing okay."

"Me too. Let's try using our goddess powers to send them happy-hugs back," suggested Persephone. So saying, she wrapped her arms around herself in a big hug.

Aphrodite did the same. "Now what?" she asked.

Persephone made up a chant. After she'd taught it to Aphrodite, they squeezed their eyes shut and spoke it together in singsong voices:

"We wish we might, we wish we may,
send lucky hugs to our friends far away."
Then they each opened their

arms wide and set their hugs free to fly away. Wherever Artemis and Athena were right now, Persephone knew they'd feel the good wishes she and Aphrodite had just sent. And maybe the hugs would help them in their jewel quests, too.

"I'll be glad when we finally meet Athena and Artemis again in Sparkle City," said Persephone. "It's fun all hanging out together."

Aphrodite nodded. "It'll be great to hear about their adventures. And to tell them about ours!" She began skipping over the orange and blue bricks to hop from one pink brick to another as they went down the road.

Persephone skipped along beside her. She knew that she and Aphrodite would do their very best to find the missing emerald. And she felt in her heart that no matter what trouble they met on their adventure to the Kingdom of Cut-Ups, it would only make their friendship even stronger.

Up ahead Persephone spotted

the waving flags and towers of the kingdom. "*Hmm.* Cut-Ups. Why do you think this kingdom is named that?"

They began making silly "what if" guesses about what they'd find in the Kingdom of Cut-Ups. "What if it's a barbershop kingdom where they give silly haircuts?" "What if the Cut-Ups are creatures that cut in line all the time?" "What if . . . ?"

Soon they were giggling nonstop, as best friends often do.

Word List

accident (AK•sih•dent): A mistake that hurts someone or something

alarm (uh•LARM): Fear and worry

diamond (DI•muhnd): A beautiful clear jewel

emerald (EM•er•uhld): A beautiful green jewel

gods: Boys or men with magic powers in Greek mythology

goddess (GOD•ess): A girl or woman with magic powers in Greek mythology

Greece (GREES): A country on the continent of Europe

Greek mythology (GREEK mith•AH•luh•jee): Stories people in Greece made up long ago to explain things they didn't understand about their world

invisible (in•VIZZ•ih•bull): Something that cannot be seen

jewels (JOOLZ): Beautiful costly stones often made into rings or necklaces

mermaid (MER•mayd): A magical

woman with a fish tail who lives in the sea

mortal (MOR•tuhl): Human

Mount Olympus (MOWNT oh•LIHM•puss): Tallest mountain in Greece

pearl (PERL): A beautiful jewel found inside an oyster

ruby (RU•bee): A beautiful red jewel

sparkle (SPAR•kuhl): Shine bright

statue (STACH•oo): Carved figure of a person or animal

Thunderbolt Tower (THUHN•der•bolt TOW•er): Where Zeus lives in Sparkle City

Questions

1. What do you worry about? Homework? Grades? Making friends? What are ways you can calm your fears and worries? What could you say to a friend to calm her or his fears?

2. Imagine some super-silly worries that different creatures might have. Can you draw a picture of those worries? And then draw the creatures fighting off the worries?

3. Persephone thinks it's more fun to do things with friends than to

do things alone. What are some activities you like to do with friends? What are some activities you like to do alone?

4. Persephone and Aphrodite have a hard time sharing Adonis at first. What things are hard for you to share with others? What have you shared with someone else that made you feel good?

5. What adventures might Persephone and Aphrodite have as they search for the emerald in the Kingdom of Cut-Ups?

Authors' Note

This book is a fun adventure twist on an old Greek myth. Adonis was a supercute and popular **mortal** boy. The goddesses Aphrodite and Persephone both liked him a lot. They fought over who would get to be his best friend. Zeus decided that the two goddesses should learn to share. From then on, Aphrodite got to hang out with Adonis in fall and winter. Persephone got to hang out with him in spring and summer.

Ancient Greeks had celebrations for Adonis each year. They believed that offering small gifts to Persephone and Adonis would help their crops grow in the spring.

We hope you enjoy reading all the Little Goddess Girls books!

—*Joan Holub and Suzanne Williams*